Hello, Cy!

Amy DeLashmutt

Illustrated by Sarah Torgeson

www.mascotbooks.com

Hi, my name is Cy.

I love my job as Iowa State University's mascot and there are so many reasons why! Let me show you.

I love hearing "The Bells of Iowa State" chime from the Campanile.

Happy Birthday to You.
Happy Birthday to You.
Happy Birthday to ISU.
Happy Birthday to You.

Iowa State is celebrating its 150th birthday. Wow, that's a lot of candles. Let's celebrate on the steps of Beardshear Hall right in the heart of campus. I'll bring the balloons!

I love birthday parties! Don't you?

When I need a quiet
place to study, I take a break at the
Parks Library. It's a great place to read a
book or catch up with Cyclone fans.

The Memorial Union is one of my favorite places at ISU. There's so much to do in the MU!

I can go bowling, see works of art, create my own project in the Workspace or get something to eat.

Welcome!

owa State
niversity
ook Store

The Iowa State University Book Store inside
the Memorial Union is a great place to shop!
I can get all kinds of Cyclone t-shirts, hats,
sweatshirts and even books about Iowa State.

There are my friends, the swans, going for a swim on Lake LaVerne.

Hi, Sir Lancelot and Elaine!

Lake LaVerne is a favorite spot on ISU's campus. Past Iowa Staters might have ice skated here or been part of the canoe races during VEISHEA.

"What is that tall structure?" many Cyclones ask. Why it's the Marston Water Tower. That's right, a water tower right here on campus.

The Marston Water Tower is 168 feet tall. That's really tall. It supplied water to campus in its early days and was the first steel water tower west of the Mississippi River.

There are so many neat things to see on ISU's campus!

Reiman Gardens is one of the most beautiful places at ISU. I can see all of my favorite flowers or take a break before the next big Cyclone game. Even mascots have to rest before a big game.

Don't forget to visit the indoor butterfly wing and meet all sorts of unique and interesting butterfly friends.

Hilton Coliseum! The place where Cyclone athletes create what we fans call some "Hilton Magic."

Don't forget to yell, "Go, Cyclones!" and give me a high-five when you see me.

There's nothing better than cheering for the football team in Jack Trice Stadium. I'm the biggest Cyclone fan of them all.

Go, Cyclones!

From the Campanile to Jack Trice Stadium, and many landmarks in between, Iowa State University is a beautiful place. I hope some of these are your favorite spots, too.

To a mascot like me, Iowa State is more than just a University - it's my home.

Go, Iowa State! Go, Cyclones!

To Maddie and Aaron - my biggest fans.
~ Amy DeLashmutt

Dedicated to Tim and my family for their love and support. Thank you to the Iowa State University Book Store for this great opportunity. ~ Sarah Torgeson

For more information about our products, please visit us online at www.mascotbooks.com.

For more information, please contact Mascot Books,
P.O. Box 220157, Chantilly, VA 20153-0157

ISBN: 978-1-932888-53-9

Printed in the United States.

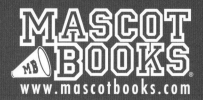

Title List

Team	Book Title	Author	Team	Book Title	Author
Baseball			**Pro Football**		
Boston Red Sox	Hello, Wally!	Jerry Remy	Carolina Panthers	Let's Go, Panthers!	Aimee Aryal
Boston Red Sox	Wally And His Journey Through Red Sox Nation!	Jerry Remy	Dallas Cowboys	How 'Bout Them Cowboys!	Aimee Aryal
New York Yankees	Let's Go, Yankees!	Yogi Berra	Green Bay Packers	Go, Packres, Go!	Aimee Aryal
New York Mets	Hello, Mr. Met!	Rusty Staub	Kansas City Chiefs	Let's Go, Chiefs!	Aimee Aryal
St. Louis Cardinals	Hello, Fredbird!	Ozzie Smith	Minnesota Vikings	Let's Go, Vikings!	Aimee Aryal
Philadelphia Phillies	Hello, Phillie Phanatic!	Aimee Aryal	New York Giants	Let's Go, Giants!	Aimee Aryal
Chicago Cubs	Let's Go, Cubs!	Aimee Aryal	New England Patriots	Let's Go, Patriots!	Aimee Aryal
Chicago White Sox	Let's Go, White Sox!	Aimee Aryal	Seattle Seahawks	Let's Go, Seahawks!	Aimee Aryal
Cleveland Indians	Hello, Slider!	Bob Feller	Washington Redskins	Hail To The Redskins!	Aimee Aryal
			Coloring Book		
			Dallas Cowboys	How 'Bout Them Cowboys!	Aimee Aryal
College					
Alabama	Hello, Big Al!	Aimee Aryal	Michigan State	Hello, Sparty!	Aimee Aryal
Alabama	Roll Tide!	Ken Stabler	Minnesota	Hello, Goldy!	Aimee Aryal
Arizona	Hello, Wilbur!	Lute Olsen	Mississippi	Hello, Colonel Rebel!	Aimee Aryal
Arkansas	Hello, Big Red!	Aimee Aryal	Mississippi State	Hello, Bully!	Aimee Aryal
Auburn	Hello, Aubie!	Aimee Aryal	Missouri	Hello, Truman!	Todd Donoho
Auburn	War Eagle!	Pat Dye	Nebraska	Hello, Herbie Husker!	Aimee Aryal
Boston College	Hello, Baldwin!	Aimee Aryal	North Carolina	Hello, Rameses!	Aimee Aryal
Brigham Young	Hello, Cosmo!	LaVell Edwards	North Carolina St.	Hello, Mr. Wuf!	Aimee Aryal
Clemson	Hello, Tiger!	Aimee Aryal	Notre Dame	Let's Go, Irish!	Aimee Aryal
Colorado	Hello, Ralphie!	Aimee Aryal	Ohio State	Hello, Brutus!	Aimee Aryal
Connecticut	Hello, Jonathan!	Aimee Aryal	Oklahoma	Let's Go, Sooners!	Aimee Aryal
Duke	Hello, Blue Devil!	Aimee Aryal	Oklahoma State	Hello, Pistol Pete!	Aimee Aryal
Florida	Hello, Albert!	Aimee Aryal	Penn State	Hello, Nittany Lion!	Aimee Aryal
Florida State	Let's Go, 'Noles!	Aimee Aryal	Penn State	We Are Penn State!	Joe Paterno
Georgia	Hello, Hairy Dawg!	Aimee Aryal	Purdue	Hello, Purdue Pete!	Aimee Aryal
Georgia	How 'Bout Them Dawgs!	Vince Dooley	Rutgers	Hello, Scarlet Knight!	Aimee Aryal
Georgia Tech	Hello, Buzz!	Aimee Aryal	South Carolina	Hello, Cocky!	Aimee Aryal
Illinois	Let's Go, Illini!	Aimee Aryal	So. California	Hello, Tommy Trojan!	Aimee Aryal
Indiana	Let's Go, Hoosiers!	Aimee Aryal	Syracuse	Hello, Otto!	Aimee Aryal
Iowa	Hello, Herky!	Aimee Aryal	Tennessee	Hello, Smokey!	Aimee Aryal
Iowa State	Hello, Cy!	Amy DeLashmutt	Texas	Hello, Hook 'Em!	Aimee Aryal
James Madison	Hello, Duke Dog!	Aimee Aryal	Texas A & M	Howdy, Reveille!	Aimee Aryal
Kansas	Hello, Big Jay!	Aimee Aryal	UCLA	Hello, Joe Bruin!	Aimee Aryal
Kansas State	Hello, Willie!	Dan Walter	Virginia	Hello, CavMan!	Aimee Aryal
Kentucky	Hello, Wildcat!	Aimee Aryal	Virginia Tech	Hello, Hokie Bird!	Aimee Aryal
Louisiana State	Hello, Mike!	Aimee Aryal	Virginia Tech	Yea, It's Hokie Game Day!	Frank Beamer
Maryland	Hello, Testudo!	Aimee Aryal	Wake Forest	Hello, Demon Deacon!	Aimee Aryal
Michigan	Let's Go, Blue!	Aimee Aryal	West Virginia	Hello, Mountaineer!	Aimee Aryal
			Wisconsin	Hello, Bucky!	Aimee Aryal
NBA					
Dallas Mavericks	Let's Go, Mavs!	Mark Cuban			
Kentucky Derby					
Kentucky Derby	White Diamond Runs For The Roses	Aimee Aryal			

More great titles coming soon!

info@mascotbooks.com